The Lighthouse Keeper's Lunch

Ronda and David Armitage

SCHOLASTIC

For Joss and Kate

First published in the UK in 1977 by Andre Deutsch Ltd
This edition first published in 2017 by Scholastic Children's Books
Euston House, 24 Eversholt Street
London NW1 1DB
a division of Scholastic Ltd
www.scholastic.co.uk
London ~ New York ~ Toronto ~ Sydney ~ Auckland
Mexico City ~ New Delhi ~ Hong Kong

ISBN 978 1407 15966 9

Printed in China

3 5 7 9 10 8 6 4 2

The Lighthouse Keeper's Lunch

Ronda and David Armitage

Once there was a lighthouse keeper called Mr Grinling.
At night time he lived in a small white cottage perched high
on the cliffs. In the day time he rowed out to his lighthouse
on the rocks to clean and polish the light.

Mr Grinling was a most industrious lighthouse keeper. Come rain…

...or shine, he tended his light.

Sometimes at night, as Mr Grinling lay sleeping in his warm bed, the ships would toot to tell him that his light was shining brightly and clearly out to sea.

Each morning while Mr Grinling polished the light Mrs Grinling worked in the kitchen of the little white cottage on the cliffs concocting a delicious lunch for him.

Once she had prepared the lunch she packed it into
a special basket and clipped it on to the wire that ran from
the little white cottage to the lighthouse on the rocks.

But one Monday something terrible happened.
Mrs Grinling had prepared a particularly appetising lunch.
She had made…

A Mixed Seafood Salad

A Lighthouse Sandwich

Cold Chicken Garni

Sausages and Crisps

Peach Surprise

Iced Sea Biscuits

Drinks and Assorted Fruit

She put the lunch in the basket
as usual and sent it down the wire.

But the lunch did not arrive.
It was spotted by three scavenging
seagulls who set upon it and
devoured it with great gusto.

"Clear off, you varmints," shouted
Mr Grinling, but the seagulls took
not the slightest notice.

That evening Mr and Mrs Grinling decided on a plan to baffle the seagulls.
"Tomorrow I shall tie the napkin to the basket," said Mrs Grinling.
"Of course, my dear," agreed Mr Grinling, "a sound plan."

On Tuesday evening Mr and Mrs Grinling racked their brains for another plan.
"They are a brazen lot, those seagulls," said Mrs Grinling.
"Brazen indeed," said Mr Grinling, "what shall we do?"
"Our cat does not appear to like seagulls," said Mrs Grinling.
"No, my dear," said Mr Grinling, "Hamish is an accomplished
seagull chaser."
"Of course," exclaimed Mrs Grinling,
"tomorrow Hamish can guard the lunch."
"A most ingenious plan," agreed Mr Grinling.

Hamish did not think that this plan was ingenious at all.
He spat and hissed as Mrs Grinling secured him in the basket.
"There, there, Hamish," said Mrs Grinling consolingly,
"I'll have a tasty piece of herring waiting for you
when you arrive home."

Sadly, flying did not agree with Hamish. His fur stood on end when the
basket swayed, his whiskers drooped when he peered down at the wet,
blue sea and he felt much too sick even to notice the seagulls, let alone
scare them away from the lunch.

"Lackaday, lackaday,"
said Mr Grinling sadly.
"Miaow, miaow," agreed Hamish pitifully.

On Wednesday evening Mr and Mrs Grinling racked their brains again for a new plan. "What shall we do?" said Mr Grinling. Mrs Grinling looked thoughtful. "I have it!" she exclaimed. "Just the mixture for hungry seagulls."

"Indeed, my dear," said Mr Grinling. "What have you in mind?" "Wait and see," said Mrs Grinling, "just wait and see."

"Mustard sandwiches," chuckled Mr Grinling.
"A truly superb plan my dear, truly superb."

On Thursday morning
Mrs Grinling carefully packed
the mustard sandwiches and
sent them off down the wire
to the expectant seagulls.

On Friday Mrs Grinling repeated the mustard mixture.

So, on Saturday, up in the little white cottage on the cliffs, a jubilant Mrs Grinling put away the mustard pot before she prepared a scrumptious lunch for Mr Grinling.

While he waited for his lunch down in the lighthouse on the rocks,
Mr Grinling sang snatches of old sea shanties as he surveyed the
coastline through his telescope…

"Ah well, such is life," mused Mr Grinling as he sat down to enjoy a leisurely lunch in the warm sunshine.